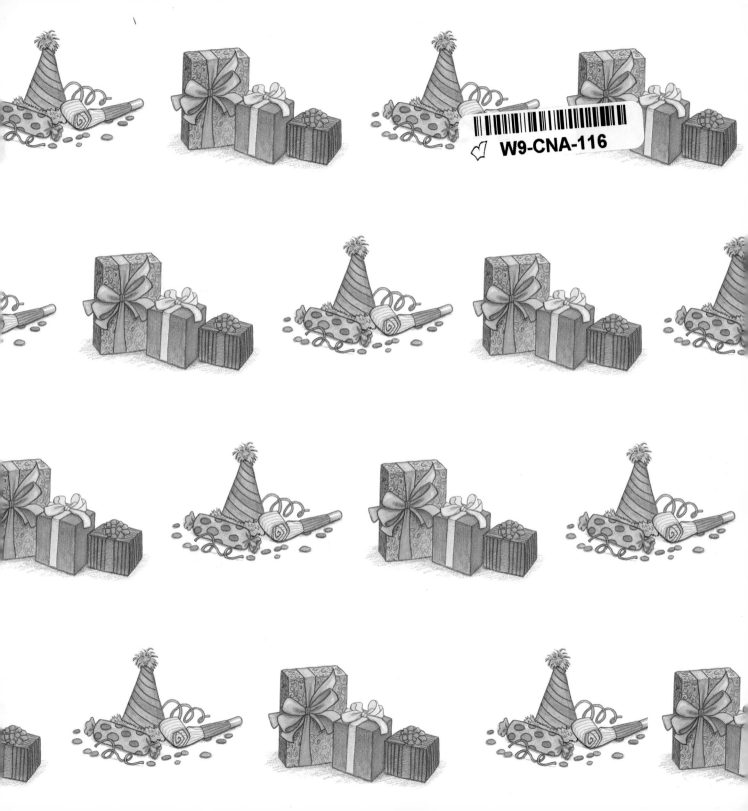

W9-CNA-116

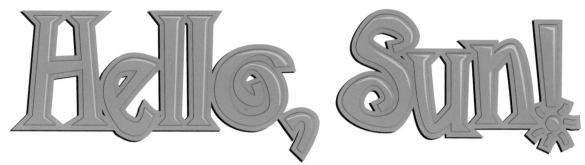

Hello, Sun!

A Morningtime Tale
of God's Great Care

By Sheila Walsh Art by Deborah Maze

A CHILDREN OF FAITH BOOK *published by* WATERBROOK PRESS

HELLO, SUN!
PUBLISHED BY WATERBROOK PRESS
2375 Telstar Drive, Suite 160
Colorado Springs, Colorado 80920
A division of Random House, Inc.

All Scripture quotations are taken from the *Holy Bible, New International Version* ®.
NIV ®. Copyright © 1973, 1978, 1984 by the International Bible Society. Used by
permission of Zondervan Publishing House. All rights reserved.

ISBN 1-57856-337-2

Copyright © 2001 by Sheila Walsh

Illustrations © 2001 by Deborah Maze

Published in association with the literary agency of Alive Communications, Inc.,
7680 Goddard Street, Suite 200, Colorado Springs, CO 80920.

Children of Faith, 402 BNA Drive, Suite 600, Nashville, TN 37217

All rights reserved. No part of this book may be reproduced or
transmitted in any form or by any means, electronic or mechanical,
including photocopying, recording, or by any information storage
and retrieval system, without permission in writing from the publisher.

WATERBROOK and its deer design logo are registered trademarks
of WaterBrook Press, a division of Random House, Inc.

Visit Children of Faith at http://childrenoffaith.com

Library of Congress Cataloging-in-Publication Data
Walsh, Sheila, 1956-
   Hello, sun! / by Sheila Walsh; art by Deborah Maze.
     p. cm.
   Summary: When God ignores her prayer for a sunny day on her birthday, five-year-old
Emma is disappointed, but then she receives a wonderful surprise.
   ISBN 1-57856-337-2
   [1. Birthdays—Fiction. 2. God—Fiction. 3. Stories in rhyme.] I. Maze, Deborah, ill. II.
Title.

   PZ8.3.W1937 Hf 2001
   [E]—dc21   2001039015

Printed in the United States of America
2001—First Edition

10 9 8 7 6 5 4 3 2 1

The LORD God is a sun and shield.

PSALM 84:11

Good morning, little happy face!
Have I a tale for you
of a birthday prayer
and an "Is God there?"
from the great land of Gnoo.

"Good morning, Sun!" little Emma said.
"Today will be finer than Mama's fresh bread!
I'm finally five and the whole world is mine!
What a day for my party! God made the sun shine."

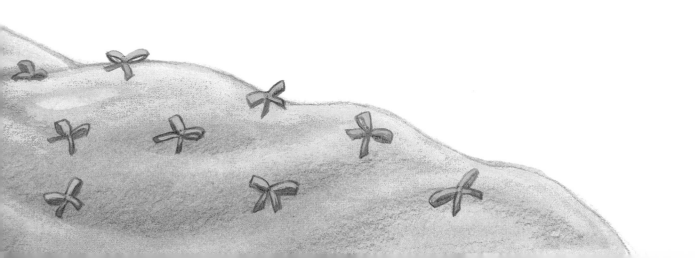

"I think I'll wear lilac. No! Blue would be best."
She pulled out her ribbons and left quite a mess.
"But pink is so pretty. I love yellow, too.
I'll wear every one of them—that's what I'll do!"

She ran down the stairs,
taking two at a time.
  She barked like a puppy,
  then roared like a lion.
    "Hello, darling Daddy
    and Mama and Ben!"
      She kissed her dog,
      Princess, again and again.

"Today will be perfect. The sun is so bright.
I asked God for sunshine, not showers, last night.
We'll dance 'round the apple tree, then for a treat
we'll sit on the grass and we'll eat, eat, eat, eat!"

"The weatherman says it will rain," Daddy said.
"By lunchtime the sun might be hiding its head.
But we'll all have such fun. Let it rain, sleet,
  or snow!
My baby is five! Well, where did the years go?"

"But I asked God for sun. I was very specific.
To see it rain now—why, the thought is horrific!
It would ruin my party, one drop at a time.
I asked God for sunshine, so sunshine is mine!"

But soon black and stormy clouds painted the sky.

Emma looked out of the window and cried.

The puddles grew bigger, then bigger than big.

The wind shook the apple tree, jiggety jig.

"I'm not going to pray anymore!" she declared.

"I asked God for sunshine. I don't think he cares.

Perhaps he's forgotten today is my day.

I'm angry and sad. That's all I can say!"

"Come here, little angel. Come sit on my knee,
and Daddy will rock like a boat on the sea.
I know that you're sad, but I know this is true:
God didn't forget you. He really loves you."

"Perhaps there's a little boy, not far away,
who asked God for rain on this very same day.
Or a farmer who needs rain to fall on his corn.
Or a family of ducks who were feeling too warm."

"But God loves you more than a daddy can tell.
He heard every prayer; not a single one fell.
And whether we've sunshine or snowfall or sleet,
today will be perfect with your dancing feet!"

He prayed with his daughter and said an amen,
then the clouds in the sky started moving again.
Emma ran to the window as fast as could be
to see if the sun had returned to her tree.

"Oh, Daddy! Come look at this wonderful sight.
All the colors I love! You must have been right.
What a wonderful gift! It's from God, I just know.
He has sent me a beautiful birthday rainbow."

It was just for a time, then the sun went away
and the clouds on the apple tree stayed for the day.
But she splashed in the puddles again and again
with Princess and Teddy and all her best friends.

"Did the boy see the rainbow? The man in his corn?
Did the ducks see my present reflect in their pond?
And thank you, dear Daddy, for helping me know
whether sunshine or puddles, God loves me so!"

Our story has ended.
What a happy tale too!
Would you like a party
in the land of Gnoo?